D1507469

Henry Herz | Illustrations by Luke Graber

# GOOD EGG AND BAD APPLE

Schiffer
Publishing Ltd
4880 Lower Valley Road • Atglen, PA 19310

**Other Schiffer Books by Henry Herz:**
*Mabel and the Queen of Dreams,*
ISBN: 978-0-7643-5137-2

**Other Schiffer Books on Related Subjects:**
*The Cycling Wangdoos* by Kelly Pulley,
ISBN: 978-0-7643-5406-9
*Wind and Oyster Jack* by Marcia Moore,
ISBN: 978-0-7643-5422-9
*Bicyling Rules of the Road: The Adventures of Devin Van Dyke* by Kelly Pulley, ISBN: 978-0-7643-5328-4

Designed by Henry Herz & Luke Graber
Cover design by Brenda McCallum
Type set in Americana BT/Brandon Grotesque

ISBN: 978-0-7643-5603-2
Printed in China

Published by Schiffer Publishing, Ltd.
4880 Lower Valley Road
Atglen, PA 19310
Phone: (610) 593-1777; Fax: (610) 593-2002
E-mail: Info@schifferbooks.com
Web: www.schifferbooks.com

For our complete selection of fine books on this and related subjects, please visit our website at www.schifferbooks.com. You may also write for a free catalog.

Schiffer Publishing's titles are available at special discounts for bulk purchases for sales promotions or premiums. Special editions, including personalized covers, corporate imprints, and excerpts, can be created in large quantities for special needs. For more information, contact the publisher.

We are always looking for people to write books on new and related subjects. If you have an idea for a book, please contact us at proposals@schifferbooks.com.

*With thanks to my wife, parents,*
*and the Author of all things.*

Bad Apple snuck up on Romaine.
"Boo!"

Romaine wilted in fear.
The vegetables were steamed.

But not Second Banana.

"That looks like fun! C'mon, let's go stalk Celery."

After taunting Celery, Bad Apple tipped over Half & Half.

"Ha! No use cryin' over spilt milk."

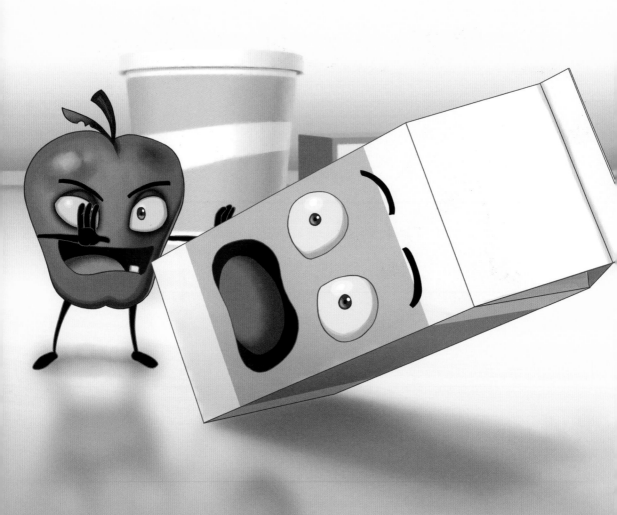

"Look," Good Egg whispered to his best friend. "Bad Apple's spoiling other food."

"He's rotten to the core. Why?" asked Zucchini.

"Sour Grapes called him names," replied Good Egg. "They won't play with him. They pushed him around. Now he's mean to others. C'mon, let's go help Half & Half."

"Uh oh, here comes Bad Apple.
Quick, hide!" urged Good Egg.

Zucchini ducked behind the tortellini.
Good Egg hid behind the napping Sweet Potato.

"Well, if it isn't teenie weenie Zucchini. Let's squash him!" said Bad Apple.

"I've got a better idea," said Second Banana.

He yanked up Zucchini's plastic wrap.
"Ha! A veggie-wedgie!"

Sweet Potato woke up. Bad Apple scowled at her.
She turned to flee but bumped into Second Banana.

"Don't run off half-baked," he scolded.
Bad Apple shoved Sweet Potato.
Sweet Potato fought back tears.
"Boo, hoo. Look who's thin-skinned,"
said Second Banana.

The fruits left to make mischief elsewhere.

"It's okay, Sweet Potato," said Good Egg. "Maybe standing up to them will stop their bullying. Just don't let them sneak up on you."

"Okay, I'll keep my eyes peeled."

"Watch out! They're coming back," warned Sweet Potato.
Good Egg rolled in front of her.
"Outta my way!" ordered Bad Apple.
Good Egg wobbled but stood his ground. "I'm not scared."

"Well, you oughtta be," replied Second Banana.
"No one'll save your bacon."

Second Banana lunged at Good Egg but slipped on his peel. Bruised and embarrassed, he split.

Bad Apple spun Good Egg around and around.
"Ha, you're scrambled now."

"C'mon, guys," called Zucchini. "Good Egg's our friend. Let us help him."

"Hiding didn't work. Standing up to Bad Apple didn't work. What else can we try?" whispered Zucchini.

"I have an idea," replied Good Egg.
"Just follow my lead."

"Knock, knock" said Good Egg.
Bad Apple glared. "Who's there?"
"Omelette."
"Omelette who?"
"Omelette smarter than I look."

The beginning of a grin formed on
Bad Apple's face.

Good Egg winked at Zucchini.

"We're gonna play capture the flag. Do you wanna play?"
Zucchini asked Bad Apple.

"Me?"

"Sure. You're strong and fast. You can be a team captain."

"Really?" Bad Apple smiled his first true smile. "Who wants to be on my team?" he asked.

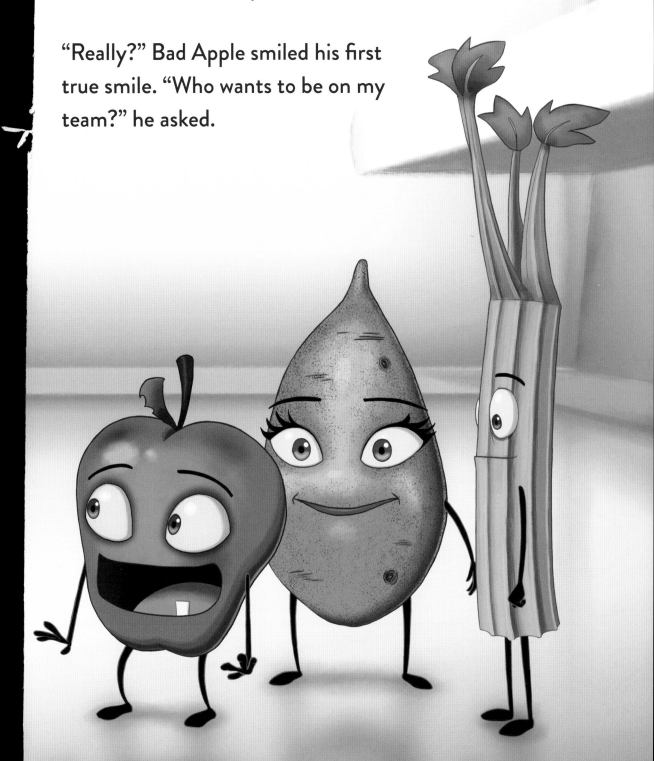

"Me," replied Good Egg.

The foods formed two teams and played the rest of the afternoon.

Good Egg and Bad Apple's team won, but everyone had fun.

But that was just icing on the cake, because
Bad Apple never bullied again.

# AUTHOR'S NOTE

An idiom is an expression not meant to be interpreted literally, such as "jump the gun" for starting too soon. A pun is the use of a word with more than one meaning. This book includes a buffet of food-based wordplay (oops, I did it again):

**Good Egg** – an idiomatic expression meaning a nice person.

**Bad Apple** – an idiomatic expression meaning a mean person.

**Second Banana** – an idiomatic expression meaning someone playing a support role; a sidekick.

**Romaine wilted** – wilt means both to droop (as picked lettuce does) and to lose self-assurance (as a bullied kid might).

**The other vegetables were steamed** – steamed means both to cook over boiling water, and to become angry.

**Let's go stalk Celery** – celery stems are stalks, and stalk also means to hunt.

**No use crying over spilt milk** – an idiomatic expression meaning not to worry about something you cannot change, combined with milk literally being spilled.

**Rotten to the core** – rotten to the core is an idiomatic expression meaning a bad person that also references the core of an apple.

**Well, if it isn't Zucchini. Let's squash him** – squash means to smash, and Zucchini is a variety of summer squash.

**Don't run off half-baked** – half-baked is an idiomatic expression meaning starting before one is ready, combined with a baked potato pun.

**Look who's thin-skinned** – thin-skinned is an idiom meaning overly sensitive, combined with a potato skin pun.

**I'll keep my eyes peeled** – eyes peeled is an idiomatic expression meaning to stay alert, combined with two potato puns. Removing the skin is called peeling a potato. Roots sprouting from a potato are called its eyes.

**No one'll save your bacon** – save your bacon is an idiomatic expression meaning to rescue you.

**Slipped on his peel** – banana peels are slippery when stepped on; a common visual joke.

**Second Banana split** – split means to leave, and a banana split is a dessert made with ice cream and bananas.

**Ha, you're scrambled now** – scrambled means to be confused or dizzy, and scrambled is one form of cooked eggs.

**Let us help him** – an auditory food pun: let us vs. lettuce. Bonus visual pun: the Swiss cheese remains neutral just like Switzerland.

**Omelette smarter than I look** – a pun on "I'm a lot" that also references eggs.

**But that was just icing on the cake** – icing on the cake is an idiomatic expression for receiving a secondary benefit that also references cake.

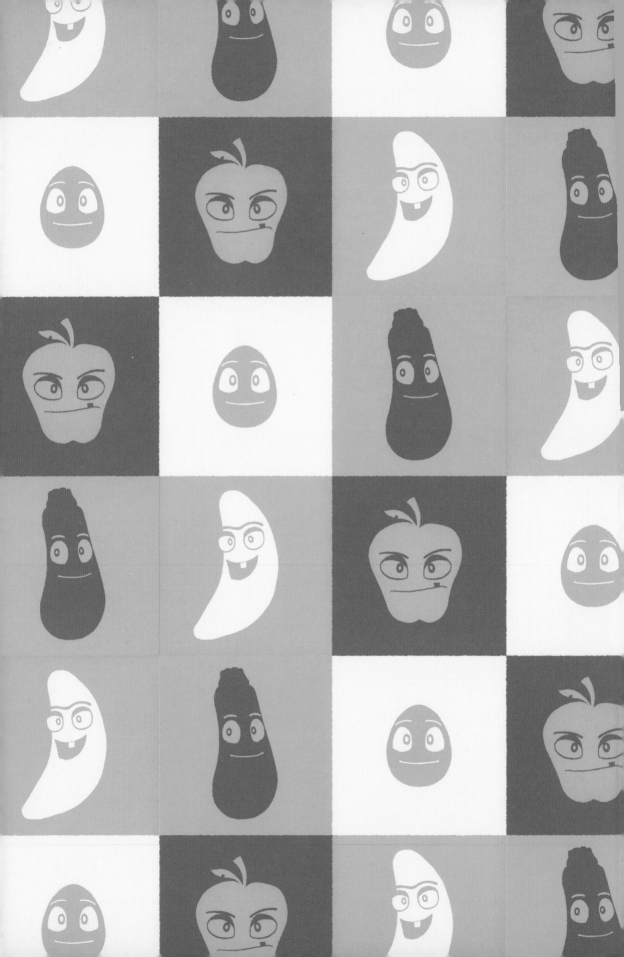